DRAGONBORN
Fangs in the Mirror

BY MICHAEL DAHL
ILLUSTRATED BY LUIGI AIME

STONE ARCH
BOOKS™

ZONE BOOKS ARE PUBLISHED BY
STONE ARCH BOOKS
A CAPSTONE IMPRINT
1710 ROE CREST DRIVE
NORTH MANKATO, MINNESOTA 56003
WWW.CAPSTONEPUB.COM

LIBRARY OF CONGRESS CATALOGING-IN-PUBLICATION DATA
DAHL, MICHAEL.
FANGS IN THE MIRROR / WRITTEN BY MICHAEL DAHL ; ILLUSTRATED BY LUIGI AIME.
P. CM. -- (DRAGONBORN)

SUMMARY: ERIK HAS NIGHTMARES ABOUT DRAGONS, AND HE IS SHOCKED WHEN HE LOOKS IN
THE MIRROR AND SEES A DRAGON FACE--BUT WHEN A GIRL NAMED VIOLET ASKS HIM TO HELP
FIND HER BROTHER HE LEARNS THE SECRET OF THE DRAGON BIRTHMARK.

ISBN 978-1-4342-4042-2 (LIBRARY BINDING) -- ISBN 978-1-4342-4255-6 (PBK.) -- ISBN 978-1-
4342-4623-3 (EBOOK)
1. DRAGONS--JUVENILE FICTION. 2. BROTHERS AND SISTERS--JUVENILE FICTION. [1. DRAGONS--
FICTION. 2. SECRETS--FICTION. 3. BROTHERS AND SISTERS--FICTION.] I. AIME, LUIGI, ILL. II. TITLE.
PZ7.D15134FAN 2012
813.54--DC23   2012004511

ART DIRECTOR: KAY FRASER
GRAPHIC DESIGNER: HILARY WACHOLZ
PRODUCTION SPECIALIST: KATHY MCCOLLEY

PHOTO CREDITS:
SHUTTERSTOCK: CAESART (METAL PLATE, PP. 1, 4, 66); FERNANDO CORTES (DRAGON PATTERN)

PRINTED IN THE UNITED STATES OF AMERICA IN NORTH MAKATO, MINNESOTA.
042012
006682CGF12

TABLE OF CONTENTS

A NEW AGE OF DRAGONS HAS BEGUN.

DRAGONBORN

Young people around the world have discovered that dragon blood flows in their veins. They are filled with new power and new ideas. But before they reveal themselves to the world, they must find one another . . .

CHAPTER 1
Nightmare

Erik had the dream again.

He was flying high above the waves.

He flew between twin moons. One real, one reflected.

The real one blazed overhead like white fire.

Its reflection gazed up at him from the water below.

Soon, he saw the shoreline. He flew toward the land.

Then, just like in every other nightmare, the moon's reflection shattered.

The surface of the water bubbled and boiled.

A mountain of ice rose from the waves. Water dripped from its sides.

Moonlight sparkled off a thousand rocks. No, not rocks. Scales.

The mountain was a vast white dragon.

Red eyes flared in the monstrous white face.

The dragon rose higher and higher.

Erik flew closer and closer to the creature.

The dragon opened its gigantic jaws.

Huge fangs glittered in the moonlight.

The fangs grew larger as Erik flew closer.

A girl's voice called for help.

Then the dragon roared.

CHAPTER 2
The Mirror

Erik awoke, sitting straight up in his bed.

Sweat covered his face and arms.

He glanced at the clock on the wall.

It was still afternoon.

Papers and books covered his bed. He had fallen asleep while doing homework before dinner.

"Erik!" his mother called from the other room. "Is everything all right?"

Erik wiped the sweat from his neck. "I'm fine," he called back. "It's nothing."

Outside, it was growing dark.

Through his window, Erik could see that streetlights had turned on.

Then Erik heard another voice outside his bedroom.

It was a voice he didn't recognize.

Someone mumbled something.

His parents were in the living room, talking with a third person.

Who?

Erik stood up and walked down the hall to the bathroom.

While he wiped his face with a cold washcloth, he tried to make out the adults' words.

"Nightmares," said his mother. Then he heard his father's voice. "All the time."

Erik wiped his face and looked in the mirror.

Then he froze.

He almost screamed.

A different face stared back at him.

A dragon's face, complete with
blazing eyes and sharp fangs.

CHAPTER 3
A Strange Question

Erik hurried to his room and shut the door.

He sat at the end of his bed, rubbing at his birthmark.

The dragon in his dreams, the same creature in the mirror, had appeared to Erik dozens of times.

But why?

"Erik," called his mother. "Could you come here, please?"

Now what? he thought.

Then he heard a noise. Erik jumped. Something was at his window.

Erik stared out cautiously.

A small stone hit the glass.

Erik opened the window.

"What —?" he started.

"Please," came a soft voice. "Don't let him hear you."

Erik was confused.

He stared out into the darkness.

"Who are you?" he demanded. "Where are you?"

A girl, his own age, stepped out from behind a tree.

"Please," she repeated. "I need your help."

Erik heard his mother's voice again. "Erik?"

"Just a minute," he yelled over his shoulder.

Then he turned back to the girl standing in his backyard.

"I need your help," she said. "It's my brother."

"I don't know you or your brother," Erik said. "I think you have the wrong house."

The girl stepped forward. "Let me ask you one question," she said. She glanced around to make sure no one else was near. Then she asked, "Do you have a birthmark that looks like a dragon?"

"Who are you?" asked Erik.

"My brother has one," said the girl. "They took him away. And I think they're going to take you away too."

"What are you talking about?" he said.

The girl stepped closer.

She looked scared.

"I can tell you what that birthmark means," she said. "But you'll have to come with me now."

Erik heard footsteps in the hall outside his room.

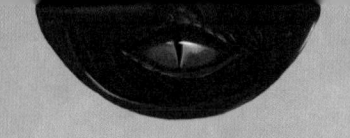

CHAPTER 4
Doctors and Dragons

He had to make a decision fast.
Should he stay where he was, or go with
the girl outside?

In two seconds he was over the sill.

He quickly lowered the window
behind him.

They ran a few steps from the house and hid behind a clump of bushes.

"What do you mean, they'll take me away?" asked Erik.

The girl's eyes glistened in the moonlight.

"My brother Chris," she said, with a wobbly voice. "He had a dragon birthmark. We have a cousin who has one, too. I just thought it was a family thing, you know."

She took a deep breath. "But it's more than that," she went on. "Our cousin disappeared. And my aunt and uncle didn't seem upset. It was like they were hiding something. And then my parents started asking Chris about his birthmark."

"Why?" asked Erik. "They're your parents. They obviously know he has it."

The girl shook her head. She began to cry softly.

"What's your name?"Erik asked.

"Violet," she said.

"Erik!" his mother called. "I have to go," said Erik.

"No!" said Violet.

Suddenly, his birthmark started to burn.

"Please," she said. "I have to tell you. My parents called a doctor about Chris. They thought the birthmark was making him sick. Giving him weird ideas. Nightmares."

Nightmares? thought Erik.

"The doctor took my brother away and I haven't seen him in weeks," said Violet.

She took a deep breath.

"My parents won't talk about it," she said. "Then today, I was riding my bike home from school, taking a shortcut, and I saw the doctor again."

"The one who took your brother?" Erik asked.

The girl nodded. She was crying harder now.

Erik felt sorry for her, but he didn't know how he could help .

He had to go inside before his parents came looking for him.

"Yes," said Violet, with a sob. "And now the doctor's inside your house."

A throb of pain shot through Erik's arm.

CHAPTER 5
The House in the Woods

"Erik! Where are you?"

It was too late to return through the window. Erik's parents were in his room.

Violet grabbed his arm.

Suddenly, the pain drained away.

"That doctor is my only connection to Chris," she said. "If I can follow him, I can find my brother. You have to help me."

Erik looked down. Why had his birthmark stopped hurting?

"Help me," Violet said again.

Then Erik recognized her voice.

It was the same as the girl's voice in his nightmare.

The girl who cried for help right before the dragon roared.

Erik heard another voice.

It was coming from the front yard.

"Don't worry," came the voice. "You can call me when Erik comes home. I'll come whenever you need me."

Violet's eyes widened. She whispered, "That's the doctor."

They crept around the side of the house.

The front door closed behind Erik's parents.

A man with gray hair got into a car.

The engine started up. The headlights turned on as the car backed out of the driveway.

"Hurry!" said Violet. "My bike's over here. We can follow him."

Erik made another quick decision. "That's too slow," he said. "Come on!"

Erik's motorcycle was parked at the side of the house.

He grabbed the handlegrips and kicked up the stand.

Silently, he pushed the bike out into the street. When they reached the corner, he jumped on and started the engine.

Violet hopped on behind him and the bike roared into the night.

It didn't take long to catch up with the doctor's car.

This is weird, Erik thought. *What am I doing out here anyway?*

But Violet had known about his dragon birthmark.

How could she have known? Why did her brother have the same mark? And why had the pain stopped when she touched him?

Soon, the doctor made a turn into a large park.

His car drove through a gate in a high stone wall. Erik shut off his headlight and followed.

He felt Violet's face near his shoulder.

"Look there," she said.

As the motorcycle drove out from under a canopy of trees, they saw a huge house at the end of the drive.

It seemed like some kind of fancy hospital.

"I think Chris must be in there," said Violet.

Erik stopped the bike and they both jumped off.

Erik stared at the monstrous beast.

Its blazing eyes stared back at him.

Then it lifted its massive head and roared.

"Where's my brother?" Violet cried.

The dragon looked at the girl.

Slowly, its talons parted and the doctor fell from its grasp.

"This is your brother," the doctor said, gasping. "I have been trying to cure him."

The man held a long syringe in one hand. "Only a few more treatments," said the doctor. "Then your brother will be normal, just like everyone else."

Several tall men ran into the room and surrounded the dragon. Each held a long-needled syringe.

The first one to reach the dragon plunged a needle into its thick purplish hide.

The dragon roared.

Violet screamed. "No!" she yelled. "There's nothing wrong with my brother!"

The dragon lowered its eyes.

A voice issued from its inhuman throat. "Violet," it seemed to whisper. "Run . . . away."

"Your brother needs help," said the doctor. "And from the look of it, he's not the only one."

He was staring at the birthmark on Erik's arm.

"There's . . . there's nothing wrong with me," said Erik.

"Really?" said the doctor. "What about those terrible nightmares. The things you see in the mirror."

"How do you know about that?" asked Erik.

"All my patients have the same problem," replied the doctor. "And I'm here to help."

Erik felt dizzy. The room seemed smaller, suddenly.

His head bumped against the ceiling.

He was growing taller and taller.

His bare arms were thick and strong.

He was covered in white scales.

His legs ended in powerful claws.

Erik turned and saw himself in a mirror.

It was the face he had seen in his dreams. The face reflected in his mirror at home.

He was the creature with burning eyes and gleaming fangs.

CHAPTER 6
Flight

"You won't take him!" shouted the doctor.

The dragon that was Erik bellowed like thunder.

His massive tail flung the other men aside.

Tables overturned and medical tools crashed to the floor.

Erik screamed again.

A stream of flame shot from his jaws.

The purple dragon roared back at Erik.

It reached out a claw and plucked Violet off the floor.

Then it turned and smashed through the windows.

Erik followed.

In the night sky, the dragons soared above the hospital.

AUTHOR

Michael Dahl is the author of more than 200 books for children and young adults. He has won the AEP Distinguished Achievement Award three times for his nonfiction. His Finnegan Zwake mystery series was shortlisted twice by the Anthony and Agatha awards. He has also written the Dragonblood series. He is a featured speaker at conferences around the country on graphic novels and high-interest books for boys.

ILLUSTRATOR

Luigi Aime was born in 1987 in Savigliano, a small Italian city near Turin. Even when he was only three years old, he loved to draw. He attended art school, graduating with honors in Illustration and Animation from the European Institute of Design in Milan, Italy.

DISCUSSION QUESTIONS

1. Which of the characters in this book have dragon blood?

2. Why was the doctor at Erik's house?

3. What questions do you still have about this story? Discuss them!

WRITING PROMPTS

1. Write a short story about Violet's brother. What do you think he is like?

2. It can be very interesting to think about a story from another person's point of view. Try writing this story, or part of it, from Violet's point of view. What does she see, hear, think, and say? What does she notice? How is the story different?

3. Create a cover for a book. It can be this book or another book you like, or a made-up book. Don't forget to write the information on the back, and include the author and illustrator names!

GLOSSARY

birthmark (BURTH-mark)—a mark on the skin that was there from birth

blazed (BLAYZD)—burned fiercely

cautiously (KAW-shuhss-lee)—with nervousness

cure (KYUR)—to make someone better

inhuman (in-HYOO-muhn)—cruel and brutal

massive (MASS-iv)—huge

monstrous (MON-struhss)—huge, frightening

recognize (REK-uhg-nize)—to know who someone is

reflection (ri-FLEK-shuhn)—an image seen in a shiny surface, like a mirror

scales (SKALEZ)—small pieces of hard skin that cover the body of a fish, snake, or other reptile

syringe (suh-RINJ)—a tube with a plunger and a hollow needle, used for giving injections

THEY MUST WORK TOGETHER TO
FIGHT THE COMING BATTLE. BUT FIRST
THEY MUST FIND EACH OTHER . . .

ERIK ROSETH

Erik has dreamed about dragons for as long as he can remember. One night, when he was eleven, he dreamed he was flying. He woke up in his neighbor's backyard. A fence surrounded the yard and the gate was locked. He had no idea how he got there. Unless . . .

Age: 17
Hometown: Charleston, South Carolina
Dragon appearance: White and Silver
Dragon species: *Draconis dentis* ("fang dragon")
Strength: Hunt and rescue

DRAGONBLOOD
RUNS THROUGH THEIR VEINS...

Find cool websites and more books like this one
at www.Facthound.com.

Just type in the Book ID: 9781434240422
and you're ready to go!

A roar ripped through the air.

The roar was a man screaming.

The sound reminded Erik of the dragon's roar in his dream.

"Did you hear that?" he asked.

Violet looked at him, confused. She shook her head.

"Come on," said Erik. "Let's find your brother."

They walked to the side of the building.

"He could be on any floor," said Erik. "I think we need to go inside."

Violet found a door and they stepped quietly inside.

Erik walked down an empty hallway.

It was oddly quiet, for a hospital.

Where are the nurses? he wondered.

Then Erik heard the scream again.

"Down here!" he yelled.

He ran down another hallway.

Violet was close behind.

Erik burst through a set of double doors.

The gray-haired stranger, the doctor, was screaming.

He was gripped in the claw of a huge, purple dragon.